THE STORY OF COLUMBUS

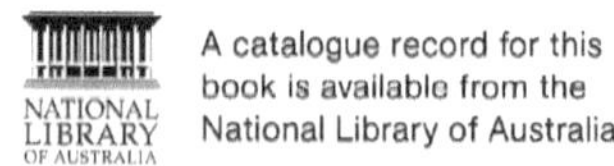

A catalogue record for this book is available from the National Library of Australia

THE STORY OF COLUMBUS

by

GLADYS M. IMLACH

GET ALL OF THE 'HISTORY SHAPERS' BOOKS
The Story of...

David Livingstone	Robert Bruce	Chalmers of New
H. M. Stanley	General Gordon	Guinea
Abraham Lincoln	Lord Clive	Bishop Patteson
Sir Francis Drake	Captain Cook	Joan of Arc
Sir Walter Raleigh	Nelson	Napoleon
Columbus	Lord Roberts	Cromwell

PLEASE NOTE

In this series, you will read about historical figures who displayed courage, bravery, self-sacrifice, and many other admirable traits. Their stories remind us that many people in history took bold actions and made tough choices. Yet, even those who achieved great things sometimes held ideas or pursued goals that were not beneficial to everyone. History is full of complex individuals—parts of their lives inspire us to be brave and stand up for what is right, while other parts remind us to consider the unintended consequences of our actions.

As you explore these biographies, we invite you to reflect on the qualities that enabled these figures to achieve greatness and the lessons we can learn from their mistakes. Maybe you too can become a History Shaper—someone who learns from the past and helps to make our world a better place for everyone.

Contents

The Unexplored Seas

In Genoa, a famous seaport of Italy, walled in by rocky mountains, Christopher Columbus was born about the year 1447. He was the eldest son of a weaver, and had three brothers and one sister. Two of these brothers, Bartholomew and Diego, especially the more daring and vigorous Bartholomew, were afterwards his companions and helpers in his great discoveries.

Their home was not far from the harbour. Very often the children must have wandered down there, and looked at the great trading ships with their white sails, and the long, narrow war-vessels with their rows of oars. And they would talk to the sailors, and hear their stories, and smell the salt sea smell. So, while Christopher was quite small, the sea mastered him and made him her own, and when he was fourteen years old he went for his first voyage.

But before this he was sent to the weavers' school, where he was soon taught to read and write. He did so well that people said of him that if he had spent his time copying letters and documents in his beautiful handwriting he would have been a rich man. He learned many other things also—arithmetic, and drawing, and painting, and Latin; and he was especially fond of studies that would help him when he became a sailor, such as geography and astronomy, the study of the stars that guide the ship by night. Even when he had left school, and had gone to sea, he made use of his spare time in learning more of these things.

Now, when Christopher Columbus went to sea, sailors did not take very long voyages. In those days, Australia and America and South Africa were not known, and the ships used to keep close to the land as they sailed from one port in France or Spain to another. The Portuguese, who were the bravest seamen of that time, had sailed some way down the west coast of Africa, but, as they had no maps to guide them, their ships were often wrecked on the unknown shores.

Men were not, however, as ignorant as they had been, for they had begun to believe that the world was round like a ball, instead of being flat like a sheet of paper. And they said to themselves, "If it is round, we should be able to sail on and on till we come back to some place we know." Then they said, "What is the most distant country we have heard of?" The answer was "Asia." So they thought, "If some one were to sail to the west over that great Atlantic Ocean, surely he would come at last to Asia." For they did not know that America lay between, and a man must come there first, as Columbus afterwards found. And no man was brave enough to try. For the Atlantic Ocean was very terrible with its storms and its unknown miles of sea, and perhaps its huge serpents and monsters; and many ship's captains said, "Ah, yes; but suppose the world were flat after all, and we came to the edge and fell over. No; we will not go."

As Columbus grew up he thought a great deal about this, and wondered continually whether any one would ever be able to sail across the Atlantic.

And he did many brave deeds. Once he went with a ship of war to Tunis, while all his men begged him to go back and ask for help; and there he captured a great foreign vessel. He took part in much of the fighting that went on in those days in the Mediterranean Sea, and he sailed to Iceland and Madeira and many other places. He said himself, "Wherever ship has sailed, there have I journeyed."

When he was about thirty years old he went to live at Lisbon, and he married a Portuguese lady, and got to know many of the Portuguese, and heard about the discoveries they were making. And he read all the books of travel he could find, and wrote to the wisest men who then lived, asking them what was known about Asia, and if they thought it could be found by sailing across the Atlantic. Some of them thought so, and they all told him it was full of gold and silver and diamonds and spices, so that he could fill his ships with riches. The wisest of all, Toscanelli, sent him a map which he had made, in which he showed Asia lying just where America is on the other side of the Atlantic, and told him to sail always to the west, for if he missed the most wonderful country,

Japan, he would come to China, or India, or some of the places marked on the map, and so would be able to direct his course. He wrote: "I perceive your magnificent and great desire to find a way to where the spices grow. I do not wonder that you, who have great courage, and all the Portuguese people, who have always been men eager for all great undertakings, should be with a burning heart and feel a great desire to undertake the said voyage."

Columbus also talked with sailors, and some of them told him stories of lands they had seen far away to the west; though, indeed, they had probably mistaken some dark ridge of cloud for land. One old man said that a long time ago he had found the bodies of two men lying on the shore, where they had been carried by the waves. They were brown and broad-faced, not like any Christian people, and must have come from an unknown country. Other seamen spoke of strange reeds and trees, and of a carved staff which had drifted from the west across the ocean. And the more Columbus thought, the surer he became that he was the man to go on this strange voyage, and that he would succeed in finding the far-off land.

So, because he was one of those men who never grow careless and lazy, nor forget any great plan they have made, he began, after many years of waiting and thinking, to look for the ship and the crew that would take him across the seas. For he was a poor man, earning his living by drawing maps, and he could not buy a ship, while no ordinary person would lend one for such a dangerous voyage. So it was long before he was able to sail. Yet all this time he was as certain of his success as if his eyes already saw the land.

In Spain

Because Columbus was living in Portugal, he went first to the King of that country and told him of his plans. King John was a wise man, and wished to have new lands to rule over, but he was also very crafty. He asked his counsellors what they thought of Columbus' proposal, and when they said it would cost too much money to send the ships he listened to them. Then he did a mean thing; he secretly sent a vessel of his own to see whether Columbus was right and there was any land beyond the ocean or no. This ship sailed out for some days, and the crew saw only the waves and the sky, and they became afraid and put back to Portugal, saying scornfully that Columbus was only a dreamer, and that of course no land was there. But when he heard of this voyage, and understood that the King had kept him at Court by false promises only to deceive him, Columbus was very angry, and swore that he would leave Portugal for ever. Then he went to the Courts of many of the princes of Europe, and even to his own city Genoa, and found faith nowhere. He sent his brother Bartholomew to our own King Henry VII. of England, but on his way the ship was captured by pirates, and poor Bartholomew was taken a prisoner to a foreign land, where he remained for a long time.

Meanwhile King John repented of his folly, and sent to Columbus and begged him to come back, promising all he had asked for. But the latter was too prudent to trust any man a second time, who had once played him false.

At last Columbus went to the Spanish Court. Ferdinand and Isabella, the King and Queen of Spain, were rich, powerful, and fortunate, and Isabella was very kind-hearted. She liked Columbus from the first, and he was a man to be liked, for he was tall and dignified, and spoke pleasantly and well. He had a fine head too, with keen blue eyes and a well-cut nose, though his hair grew white while he was still young. And he was sure of the success of his plans, and very proud, and determined that when he found the far-off lands he would not give up all the glory of their discovery to the King and Queen who had sent him. So he told them, "You must make me Admiral of your ships in the new western seas, and Viceroy, or under-king, in the lands I shall gain for you. More than that, you must give me a tenth part of all the riches I find, for I shall need money when I am great. And I wish my little son Diego and his children to have these rights when I am dead, so that the family of Columbus may be honoured for evermore."

Ferdinand and Isabella thought that Columbus asked for too great a reward, and their ministers told them that the voyage could never be made; so they hesitated instead of giving him an answer at once. Then a war broke out, and they were too busy to think of him, though he waited patiently for a long time.

When he could not bear any further delay, he resolved to go to the King of France. On the way he passed through the little port of Palos, from which he was afterwards to sail. Near this port there was an old convent. At its gate Columbus stopped to ask if he and his young son Diego, who was with him, might rest for a little. The friar who came to them readily gave permission, and brought them some bread and a pitcher of water. Columbus talked with him about his hopes, and he became so much interested that he asked the prior of the convent to listen to the strange story. The prior was delighted with Columbus and believed him, and told him not to leave Spain yet, for he would try to help him. Accordingly he sent to his friends among the merchants of Palos, and one of them, Martin Alonzo Pinzon, said he would go on the voyage, and would help to provide the ships.

The prior then rode to the Court to see the Queen, and came to her, and told her that Columbus had given up hope of Spanish help, and was setting off for France. She said, "No, he must not go, even though I sell my own jewels to get the money." And, remembering how poor he was, Isabella sent a mule for him and a costly suit of clothes, that he might not be ashamed to come to Court. When he arrived she summoned him at once, and she and Ferdinand promised that he should be Viceroy, and Admiral, and have part of the riches, if he discovered the lands across the ocean. Lest he should fear to leave his children alone in a strange land, they made Diego page to their own son Juan, and promised to take great care of Fernando, who was only four years old.

So Columbus thanked the King and Queen, and hastened back to Palos to get together ships and men for the long voyage. After all these weary years his opportunity had come.

He went to the chief magistrates of Palos and gave them the royal orders to furnish three ships for his enterprise. They marched in a procession to the great church of the town, and from its porch they read these orders to the citizens of Palos.

Then fear spread among the seamen, who said they would not come back from the rash adventure, and among the ship-owners, who thought they would lose their vessels. But Columbus' friend, the prior, reassured them, and Martin Pinzon and his brothers offered to provide one ship. The merchants dared not disobey the King's command, and the other two ships were also found. They were all small—the largest was only sixty-three feet long, the length of a short cricket-pitch—but perhaps that was a good thing, for they were needed to sail among islands and up rivers as well as on the seas; and only one, the *Santa Maria*, was completely decked, the other two, the *Pinta* and the *Niña*, merely had cabins at the prow and stern.

There was trouble with the sailors. Some tried to escape; some hid; some pretended to be ill; some had wives and mothers, who hung about the ships weeping. Columbus was forced to be harsh, and to refuse to let any stay behind; so that before he left Palos he was hated by all the poor people in the port. Besides ninety seamen, one of whom was an Englishman, and another an Irishman, there were on board some reckless young men in search of adventure, a doctor, some artisans, and some clerks,—in all about a hundred and twenty persons.

By the beginning of August all was ready, and Columbus made confession and took communion before sailing. So, too, did all the crew. Then, on Friday the 3rd of August 1492, he embarked as Admiral on the *Santa Maria*, Martin Pinzon took command of the *Pinta*, his brother of the *Niña*, and the three ships moved slowly out of Palos harbour. They had begun the great voyage.

Across the Ocean

The little fleet first steered to the south-west. At the end of the third day the *Pinta* showed signals of distress, and it was found that the rudder had been improperly secured by the owners, in order that thus the ship might be compelled to put back to Spain. Martin Pinzon, who was a cool-headed man, got a rope put round the rudder, and managed to reach the Canary Islands, where he meant to charter a new vessel and to leave the *Pinta*. But because Columbus heard that the King of Portugal, in his jealousy of the Spanish power, had sent to seize him and so to put a stop to the expedition, he dared not delay longer than was necessary for repairing the damage, and set off again on the 6th of September.

At first only light winds blew, and the vessels moved slowly over the calm sea, but when they had lost sight of land, the sailors began to be afraid. They looked around and saw everywhere the grey sea meeting the grey sky, and they wept and groaned piteously, calling out that they would never see their country and their friends again. The Admiral was much disturbed and annoyed by their cowardice, but he went among them and comforted them. He talked to them of the wonderful countries of Asia, and of the fame and riches each man would gain by his voyage, until they were all quite gay and cheerful, and busied themselves heartily with their work.

Columbus saw, however, that he would have trouble with them in the future, and that night he began to keep two log-books, a true one for himself, in which he entered the number of miles the ship had really gone every day, and a false one for the men to see, where he set down a much smaller number. For if they thought they had covered only a short distance, they would not be as impatient as if they were daily expecting the end of the voyage; and Columbus knew the way might be longer than any of them supposed. As indeed it was.

He was prudent enough to give orders to the captains of the *Niña* and the *Pinta* that if they were separated from him by storm or fog, they should sail due west for 2000 miles, and then wait, for there he hoped to find land.

He soon learned that he dared not trust his sailors to steer, for continually they let the ships fall off to the north-east. So he watched over the course of the fleet by night and day. He took charge of the instruments, the quadrant and the compass, and always made the reckoning himself. He kept a journal too, and wrote in it an account of all that happened on the way. And he prepared maps in which to draw the new lands, that all men might see exactly where he had been. It was not surprising then that, anxious and hard-working as he was, he did not rest much during the voyage; indeed, he said himself that he forgot sleep.

About the middle of September the sea was no longer barren of all interest. First a mast went floating by, and dismayed the sailors with thoughts of the lost crew and with forebodings as to their own fate. Then they saw a tern and a boatswain bird, and rejoiced, because these birds do not venture far out on the sea; but on the next day they were alarmed by a great meteor with a trailing wake of fire which fell into the sea before them. And the needle of the compass turned, pointing to the north-west, and they fancied that some evil power must be working to mislead them.

They grumbled, too, saying that it was all very well now for the wind to blow from the east, but if it did not change they could never sail back to Spain. Then they were delighted by an announcement of Pinzon's, whose boat was the lightest and the fastest, that far off he could see a low, long mist which must be land, and just as much disappointed when the supposed land turned out to be a cloud. All this time Columbus bore with them patiently, and their complaints and hopes did not affect his mind, and he still gave the sailing orders: "Westward always."

Then they saw masses of driftweed on which live crabs were floating, and flocks of birds passed overhead, but when they let down a weight to feel for a bottom, the sea was deeper than they could sound. The weeds grew thicker and thicker, until the ships could hardly make any progress, and on all sides they seemed to be surrounded by dry land.

And again the crews murmured, and declared the country was enchanted, and that the ships were caught in the weeds, and would be held fast for ever. The sun shone gloriously, the weather was wonderfully calm and mild, and three small birds perched on the rigging, and sang all day long as if they had been among fields.

At last the wind changed and blew gently from the south-west, and the Admiral was able to say that now at least they could go back whenever they wished.

Soon they left the region of the weeds, and the sailors bathed alongside the ship in the calm sea. But suddenly it rose, and heavy waves tossed the ships about, though there was little wind. This often happens in the middle of the ocean, but even Columbus had not known such a thing occur before, and he could not allay the men's fears. They began to talk openly about the risks they ran, and to mock at their leader.

"Oh yes," they said, "he thinks of nothing but being Viceroy and Admiral; he does not see that he will soon have lost his life and our lives into the bargain. He is a madman. Why should we obey him? There is little enough to eat now, and soon all our provisions will be finished. The ships are leaking too. Nobody in Spain will blame us if we bind him with cords, and tell them that under this mad leader we nearly died. Or, better still, let us throw him into the sea, and say he fell overboard while he was gazing up at the stars in his ridiculous way."

Thus they talked and wailed, but none of them was brave enough to lay his hand on the Admiral, though, if they had known it, Columbus' own heart was heavy, and he wondered how much longer he would be able to make them obey him. After a time, however, he went to them and called them his comrades, and speaking with great coolness and sweetness, reminded them that if they returned to Spain without him, their punishment would be death. And he spoke to them of the birds they had seen, which must have flown from some land near by. They were quieted for a little, but there were many weary days to pass yet.

One day at the end of September, Martin Pinzon signalled again from the *Pinta* that land was in sight on the south-west. The crews fell on their knees and thanked God. And Columbus, who hoped that he was now near Japan, climbed up the mast and watched anxiously, as the prows of the ships were turned towards it. But only a cloud was there, and despair followed their excitement.

On the 1st of October, by Columbus' own reckoning, they had crossed 2100 miles of sea, and still they were surrounded by the waves. The water was full of fish, particularly of flying fish, which leapt in and out, and flocks of birds passed overhead, but there was nothing else to interest the voyagers. A sum of money had been promised to him who first saw land, and all day long the excited men were persuading themselves that this or that cloud was some island, and startling the whole ship with their shouts. To put an end to these useless alarms, the Admiral at last declared that if any man again made a mistake, he should not have the reward, even though he were fortunate in the end. This, of course, made them all very careful.

However, on the 7th of October, the sound of a gun was heard from the *Niña*, and a flag was run up to her mast. This was the signal all had been waiting for, and the men pressed eagerly on deck. But it turned out to be the cruellest disappointment of all, and nearly ended Columbus' voyage. For when on the next day the fancied land had disappeared, the sailors on the *Santa Maria* rose up in a body and went to him, and said that they would not go farther with him, and that unless he would change the ships' course for Spain, they would find a new captain of their own to take them back. As always, he stood boldly up before them, and asked them how they dared approach him thus, saying firmly: "I will not turn back till with the help of God I find that land."

But though the men cringed before him like frightened dogs, and shuffled their feet, they were more afraid of the strange seas than they were of their Admiral, and, when he ordered them to go to their work, they remained sullenly crouching against the bulwarks, like wild, despairing animals. He saw that this time he could not master them, and for a moment his heart failed within him.

This then was to be the end of all; he had planned and worked and prayed, and given up his whole life just for a dream. And yet even now he was sure that land must be near. At last he raised his head and said very quietly, without a trace of the struggle in his mind: "Give me, my men, but three days." The men assented silently and moved away, and they worked and waited for the third day when they might turn homewards. For they had ceased to care about any fame or riches they might gain, and grudged every hour's sail to the west.

Two whole days went by, and Columbus' hopes fell lower. But on Thursday, the 11th of October, the sailors picked up a thorn-branch with fresh red berries on it, which must have been newly broken off. They found too some river weed, and a small cane cut by a man's hand. They were all excited by these discoveries, especially as Columbus had added a velvet doublet to the promised reward; and that night no man went to sleep, while the Admiral himself watched from the high poop of his vessel.

At ten o'clock, Columbus fancied he saw a light, but it disappeared before he could be sure. It seemed to reappear again, and he called to one of his officers, who saw it distinctly. As they watched, they saw that it moved a little and sometimes was hidden altogether, as though some person were carrying a torch among trees. But it was very faint, and when the crew were told of it, some of them could not distinguish it at all, and others were not certain that the glimmer must be a fire of man's making.

At last, at two o'clock, the *Pinta* discharged a gun and sent a boat to the *Santa Maria* to report that Roderigo de Triana, a man noted for his keen eyesight, had seen the outline of an island looming through the darkness. A few minutes later, as it grew lighter, Columbus himself saw the land about six miles away. The three ships stopped in their course and waited for morning, while the men sang, and leapt, or even wept, and praised God who had brought them safely through their perilous voyage.

San Salvador

When the sun rose on the 12th of October 1492, the sailors saw before them an island several miles long, covered with trees. The sea was calm, and the sky without a cloud, and they could distinguish figures coming from the woods and collecting on the shore to gaze at the strange vessels. The sails were furled and a boat lowered, and the Admiral, dressed gorgeously in red, took his seat in it. He was followed by Martin Pinzon and his brother, in whose hands were two banners embroidered with green crosses and a large F. and I. for Ferdinand and Isabella. Columbus himself held the royal standard of Spain.

As the boat neared the shore, they noticed that the plants were of strange growth with wonderfully coloured flowers, and that on the trees were many kinds of fruit they had never seen before. When they came into shallow water the natives ran back and watched the movements of the Spaniards from some distance in absolute quiet. As soon as Columbus had reached dry land, he fell on his knees and kissed the ground, calling out for joy, with tears in his eyes. His example was followed by his men, who then thanked God with him.

After the first few moments the Admiral rose, holding

the royal flag, and very solemnly he named the island San Salvador, and took possession of it in the name of the King and Queen of Spain. The Spaniards all swore that they would obey Columbus, and, because they believed the island was near India, they saluted him as Admiral and Viceroy of the Indies. The sailors who had been the rudest and roughest of the crew fell on their knees before him, and kissed his hand, begging for forgiveness. Others embraced him and asked him to give those who had shared in his perils and hardships some part of his rich reward. In fact, they treated him as if he had been a god, rather than a man. Columbus listened to them graciously and thanked them, saying that he would forget the faults of the past in the service and goodwill of the future.

Meanwhile the Indians, as the Spaniards called them, were coming nearer. Instead of being black, with woolly hair like negroes, as Columbus had expected to find them, he saw that they were reddish-brown in colour, and of fair height, with straight, coarse hair falling on their shoulders. They wore no clothing, but were painted gaily in red, white, and black, sometimes over the whole body, sometimes on the face only, with red circles round the eyes and a black stroke down the nose. They seemed to be very timid, and when one of the sailors raised his sword they turned back, but came on again when they found that he did not intend to hurt them. Some of them carried spears of hard wood, pointed by being charred in the fire, and one or two had a piece of sharp stone or a pointed bone fastened to the end; but these were not very dangerous weapons.

As they came up to the white men they uttered cries of astonishment at their colour, at their long beards, and at their clothes. Columbus learned afterwards that they thought the strangers were gods who had come down from the skies in the great winged ships. He ordered his men to hold out to them some coloured caps and glass beads, and then some little bells. With all these they were delighted, especially with the bells, which tinkled merrily in their hands. Gradually they lost all fear, and began gently to touch the garments of the Spaniards, and to point out curious things they saw to one another. One seized a sword blade with his hand and gave a great howl of pain and surprise when he found how sharp it was.

At last Columbus returned to the ships, but the natives followed him. Some swam through the waves, others went in canoes, which had been hollowed by fire out of a tree-trunk, for they had no tools to cut planks. These canoes held as many as forty men, and were rowed with short wide paddles, rather like shovels in shape.

That day and the next, men kept coming out to the ships with tame parrots in their hands, or cotton wound in skeins, or bread made from the cassava root. In exchange they were pleased with a broken piece of china, or a rusty nail, or some beads. "In fine, they took all and gave what they had with a good will."

Some of them wore little gold rings in their noses,

and these also they were quite ready to give for the new treasures. The Admiral, however, forbade his men to give anything worthless to the Indians, and when he saw the gold he put a stop to all the bargaining, telling the sailors that this metal belonged to the King of Spain and not to them. He asked the natives where they found it, and they pointed to the south and made him understand, partly by signs, partly because he had already managed to learn a few of their words, that a large island lay there in which was found so much of the yellow metal that the king had large bowls and pots made of it. Columbus was much pleased by this news. He thought the island must be near Japan, and resolved to sail there next.

Then he asked how they got the scars and marks of wounds he saw on many of their bodies. And they told him that once or twice every year a very fierce tribe of savages came from the north in canoes, and fought with them, and killed many of them, and carried others off as slaves. They asked him to stay and protect them from these enemies. But he could not do that.

He explored the island of San Salvador thoroughly. In the middle of it was a lake, and trees grew everywhere, but it did not seem to him large enough for a settlement, nor was there much gold. As the boats rowed round the coast more natives came springing out of the woods to gaze in amazement. They lifted up their arms and fell on their knees on the shore worshipping the white men, and some swam off to the boats, calling to all their friends to come and see the men from heaven, and bring them to eat and drink. Columbus ordered that all should be treated kindly, and gave presents to many before setting them on shore.

So it seemed at first that the coming of the white strangers might bring happiness to the timid, gentle natives, and not their ruin and death, as it did. Now the Indians were sorry when, after taking in fuel and water, the ships set sail for the south, and perhaps they were a little anxious about the fortunes of their seven countrymen whom Columbus had taken with him as guides.

Cuba and Hayti

On leaving San Salvador Columbus hardly knew which way to steer, so many were the islands that lay in his course. He sailed slowly among them, touching now at one and now at another, and finding everywhere the same beautiful trees and flowers and birds.

The trees were as green in October as they would have been in May here, and some were covered with blossom and others with ripe fruit, as if there were summer all the year round. Among them nightingales and other small birds were singing delightfully. In one of his letters Columbus said: "There are trees of a thousand sorts, and all have their several fruits, and I feel the most unhappy man in the world not to know them, for I am very sure that they are all valuable." Even the fish in the sea shone with a thousand colours, "blue and yellow and red and other tints, so that there was not a man who did not take great delight in seeing them." And as the Spaniards ate the new fruits, fondled the tame parrots, and breathed the air fragrant with spices, they began to believe they had come to the happiest place on earth, where there was never rain, or storm, or cold, but always sunshine and summer.

The people, too, were everywhere as gentle and friendly as they had been on San Salvador.

One day, as the Spaniards were passing among the islands, they saw a small canoe in which sat an Indian. The wind was fresh, and though the larger ships sailed steadily enough, the little canoe was tossing up and down and seemed in danger of being swamped. Columbus sent out a large boat to seize the Indian. In the canoe were a small jug of water, some cassava bread, and some red paint with which the native would smear his face before he landed. There was also a basket with some beads and coins in it, so that the Spaniards knew he must have come from San Salvador. When they took the savage on board he was quiet, but shivered with fright or cold. The Admiral spoke kindly to him, gave him some bread and treacle, and in the evening, when the sea was smooth and land was near, let him set off in his canoe. The man's eyes shone with pride and pleasure, and he told the natives of the island all about his adventure, for very soon canoes came from the shore with water and bread for the strangers. Columbus gave presents to all, a leather strap, or a string of beads; and because he found they were all fond of something sweet, he had a great jar of treacle opened for them. Then more of the savages came on board and offered him neatly-woven cotton sashes.

At another time two of the seven Indians who had been carried off from San Salvador attempted to escape in a canoe. They were immediately followed by a boat from the ship, but they gained the shelter of the woods, and the sailors were obliged to return without them. However, they came upon a strange Indian sitting alone in his canoe, and roughly bound him and carried him to the ship instead of the former captives. The Admiral sent for the man at once, put a red cap on his head, wound green glass beads round his arms, fastened little bells to his ears, and then sent him ashore to tell his fellows of his good fortune. This action pleased all the people on that island, and helped to reassure the five Indian prisoners. These the Admiral could not set free, because he needed them to speak to the other islanders in their own language.

For some time he sailed on in this way, asking at all the islands where gold was to be found, and in reply hearing of a large island in the south called Cuba, where there was abundance of the precious metal. He concluded that Cuba must be Japan, and decided to delay no longer in seeking it. After three days' sail he came there, and entered a harbour at the mouth of a deep, wide river.

The island of Cuba was much larger and more beautiful than any the Spaniards had yet seen. Inland were lofty hills covered with dense woods of pine and other tall forest trees; large rivers flowed down fertile valleys past scattered villages and little plots of cultivated land to the sea, and the coast was broken up by numerous bays and islets. Humming-birds flitted among the flowers in the forest, gorgeously glittering beetles crawled about the ground, strange scented trees, in which Columbus fancied he had found the spices of Asia, grew everywhere, and, best of all, among the rocks at the mouths of the rivers he believed he had found the pearl oyster itself.

He wished to ask the natives if this place were Japan, but alas! on his approach they all fled, and in their huts, built of palm trunks and branches, and thatched with palm leaves, the Spaniards found only some cotton cloth and some bone fishing-hooks. Martin Pinzon heard from one native whom he captured that this was no island, but a great continent stretching far to the west, and Columbus was rather pleased than disappointed, for he imagined he must have sailed past Japan and come directly to the great land of China. One of the San Salvador Indians was persuaded to go ashore and speak to the natives, who told him that the country was very large, and that beyond the hills were rich nations ruled by powerful kings. But he must have made mistakes in the language, for he said they also spoke of tribes of one-eyed men, and especially of one fierce cannibal people with dogs' noses, who fell upon their enemies and sucked their blood.

Columbus sent some of the best of his men up one of the rivers to find these great kings, and while they were away he had his ships turned over one by one on their sides, and made the sailors clean the hulls, so that they sailed as fast as when he left Spain. But when the expedition returned, they had only found a village of about fifty houses, where the people took them for gods, kissing their hands and feet, and begging them to stay there for ever.

One marvellous thing they saw—men and women putting rolls of leaves in their mouths, lighting them, and swallowing the smoke. The leaves used by these fire-eaters were named tobacco, and the Spaniards were much shocked by their daring. They said, too, that they had seen some little animals like rabbits which lived among trees, as the English squirrel does, and some large dogs which did not bark nor make any noise, but there were no horses, cows, or sheep. There were, however, a great many serpents and lizards, and the Indians ate these, and liked them as well as we do pheasants. They shot the birds, too, with arrows, and in these ways got plenty of food. One disgusted Spaniard said: "They eat all the snakes and lizards and spiders and worms that they find upon the ground, so that to my mind their bestiality is greater than that of any beast upon the surface of the earth."

When Columbus had sailed some distance along the north coast of Cuba, and had found no trace of gold, nor gathered any pearls from the oyster-shells, he decided to try the other direction and to make for a new island of which the natives continually talked to him. And he ordered the sailors to set up large crosses, made roughly of trees bound together, on every cape and headland, as a sign that the explorers brought with them the Christian faith. Sometimes, too, he would talk with the Indians about his religion.

As the ships approached the eastern point of Cuba, Martin Pinzon did a base thing. He was impatient of the

Admiral's delays, and he fancied that if he could find much gold and return to Spain with it, the glory of the voyage would be his. So one dark, stormy night he sailed away in the *Pinta* in search of the rich island he had lately heard of, thinking that if he met Columbus again he could always pretend he had been driven away by the winds against his will. But Columbus knew the envy of this man's heart, and he wrote in his journal: "Many other things also did this man do and say to me."

For some days the *Santa Maria* and the *Niña* were delayed by contrary winds. At length, on December 5, they were able to make some way to the east, and on the following day they came to Haiti.

This island was also very large, and the mountains were higher than those in Cuba. The woods did not cover the whole land, but there were open, green spaces, very fresh and beautiful, and the smoke rising in countless directions showed that there were many inhabitants. The Spaniards proceeded along the north coast, and gradually taught the natives not to fear them. On one occasion they captured a girl among the woods. They gave her some bright sashes and bells and sent her away, and soon her husband, who was the chief of that place, came in a great procession of natives to thank them. At another time a young chief ventured aboard the *Santa Maria* and dined with Columbus. He tasted each kind of food and drink eagerly, and afterwards sent an attendant for a thin gold belt, which he gave to the Admiral. In return, he accepted a gay quilt from the latter's bed, his coloured slippers, and some gold beads stamped with the pictures of Ferdinand and Isabella. At these last he marvelled, saying what great princes they must be to have sent Columbus without fear so far, even from heaven to that island.

The subjects of these chiefs came out in numbers with presents of yams, roots from which they made bread. Columbus wrote of them: "All here have a loving manner and gentle speech. Both men and women are of good stature and not black. I know they are tanned by the sun, but this does not affect them much. Their houses and villages are pretty, each with a chief who acts as their judge, and who is obeyed by them. All these lords use few words and have excellent manners. Most of their orders are given by a sign."

So far all had gone well with the adventurers, but on Christmas Day they met with their first great misfortune. The ships were in a good wide harbour, and Columbus felt that he might take a night's unbroken sleep. He gave the steersman careful instructions to keep the helm in his own hands and to watch for any sign of danger, and went to his cabin.

No sooner had the Admiral gone than the careless man called up one of the ship's boys to take his place, while he went to sleep on the deck. Gradually the *Santa Maria* drifted nearer to the shore, and the boy was not old enough to know there was danger in the sound of the breakers. She struck heavily on a reef. Columbus, roused by the shock and the boy's cries, rushed on deck, and found the *Santa Maria* lying on her side. He ordered the master and some of the sailors to take a boat and throw out an anchor astern in order to restore the ship's balance. They jumped into the boat, but, instead of obeying orders, they rowed to the *Niña* and begged to be taken aboard, crying out that the *Santa Maria* was lost.

The captain of the *Niña* refused to aid the cowards, and they were compelled to return, but too late to be of any use. The ship was settling fast, and though Columbus cut away the masts, he could not right her. Then he sent to Guacanagari, the chief of the district, and asked him for help. He immediately sent out canoes, and everything movable was taken from the *Santa Maria* and carried ashore. There it was stored in the huts, and so careful and so honest were the natives that not so much as a needle was missed. Meanwhile Guacanagari entertained the Admiral and his crew, making them many presents, and weeping over their misfortunes.

Columbus was now in a great difficulty. The small *Niña* could not hold nearly all the men, and some must be left behind. He determined to build a fort, and he chose some of the best and most active of the Spaniards to live in it till his return. He provisioned it from the wreck with bread and wine for more than a year, and bells and toys for trading, and he left there a carpenter, a gunner, a doctor, and a tailor.

As he heard that gold was found inland at a place called

Cibao, he gave orders that they should collect as much as possible during his absence. When the fort was finished he held a great ceremony and named it Navidad, and in order to show the Indians the terrible power of the white men, he fired off a salute with his largest guns. At this the natives fell to the ground, and it took some time to calm their fears and assure them of the Spanish goodwill.

About the safety of the men in the fort Columbus had no doubts. Guacanagari had learned to love him very much—he even called him his brother—and had begged for the help of the Spaniards against his enemies. There seemed nothing to fear. He wrote: "Supposing that the natives' feelings should become changed, and they should wish to injure those who have remained in the fortress, they could not do so, for they have no arms; they go naked, and are, moreover, too cowardly."

On the 4th of January 1493 the Admiral—who was very anxious lest Pinzon should reach Spain before him—left Navidad, keeping his course to the east. About two days later a sailor, who was at the masthead looking out for rocks, saw a large ship in a bay some miles off, and Columbus was glad to recognise the fugitive *Pinta*. Martin Pinzon came to him in great alarm, making many excuses for his evil conduct; and because Columbus did not wish to quarrel with the captain so far from Spain, he listened to what he had to say, and coldly declared himself satisfied with the explanation. Pinzon had collected a large quantity of gold from the natives, and he said that all the district abounded in the precious metal. But Columbus had so little trust in this man, and feared the dangers of delay so much, that he gave orders that both ships should proceed as quickly as possible.

Before they reached the eastern point of Hayti they had one more adventure. A boat's crew, which had been sent ashore for water and yams, was attacked by some fifty natives, darker and fiercer than any the Spaniards had seen before. They were Caribs—a race of cannibals of whom the other Indians stood in dread, and they used bows and arrows with some skill. Fortunately the Spaniards were able to drive off the Caribs, after killing two men. This was the first bloodshed in the New World.

The Return of the Adventurers

Columbus had intended to call at some of the smaller islands before beginning his return voyage across the Atlantic; but on the 16th of January there was such a fair wind blowing that he determined not to delay. Through this change of plans he omitted to take in ballast for his ships, and they were very ill provided against the stormy weather which followed. On one island the Spaniards saw some sea-calves, which they took for mermaids; though, as they quaintly said, they were not nearly as beautiful as the long-haired, sweet-voiced fish-women of the stories.

For the first day or two all went well; then, during the rest of January, light, baffling winds blew, and little progress was made. Soon the pilots lost their reckoning, and Columbus would not help them to find it, for he wanted to be the only man who knew the way across the seas.

About the middle of February a terrible storm arose. The *Pinta* was sailing very badly, for she had sprung her mizzenmast, and Pinzon was forced to let her run before the wind. He signalled to the Admiral as long as he could by means of lanterns, but at last the larger vessel disappeared, and the little *Niña* was alone on the sea. Great billows lifted her up and dropped her again; every time she fell into the hollow between them it seemed impossible that she should ride the next mountainous wave. She was top-heavy for want of ballast, leaking and strained, and, worst of all, the provisions, except a little bread and some peppers, had been exhausted.

Columbus took what measures he could for the common safety: to steady the *Niña* he had the empty provision-casks filled with sea-water; and he stayed at the helm himself to see that a steady hand kept the *Niña's* bows to the waves.

Fearing that none of the sailors would ever reach Spain to tell of his success, he wrote two accounts of the voyage, fastened them up in oiled paper, and enclosed each in a barrel. Thus he thought Ferdinand and Isabella might hear some day of his fortune, and be good to his family for his sake. While the sailors watched him in wonder, he cast one of the barrels into the sea, and placed the other on the poop where it would float if the ship went down.

Then he called his men together and told them to pray to God to bring them safely through this perilous voyage. They made many vows to the saints which they would fulfil if they escaped death. One was that a man should go with a great wax candle in his hand to the shrine of Our Lady of Guadaloupe. They drew lots for this by putting a bean marked with a cross among others in a bag, and Columbus drew out the marked bean. Another pilgrimage fell to him too, and a third to one of the sailors. Then together they vowed that they would all go in a procession barefoot, and in their shirts, to thank God at the first port they found.

On the 18th of February, after the storm had lasted at its worst for five days, they came in sight of land. This proved to be one of the southern islands of the Azores, which belonged to the Portuguese. Columbus allowed half his men to go ashore to perform their vow, and intended to go with the rest on their return. The men went to a chapel near the shore barefoot and in their shirts as they had vowed; but when they left the building they were surrounded by soldiers, and were told they would not be permitted to return to the ship, but would be taken to prison.

Afterwards a captain and some soldiers were sent out in a boat to seize the Admiral, but dared not venture on board the ship. Columbus threatened the officer with the King of Spain's severe displeasure, but he retorted that the Portuguese did not fear the King of Spain. In spite of the high waves, Columbus was forced to remain at sea for two days, for he could not work the *Niña* with only half his crew. He was afraid that Spain and Portugal might be at war, and he did not know what to do.

At length another boat put out from the shore with some priests on board, who said that the governor of the island wished to see Columbus' royal instructions. They were at once shown the letters of the Spanish sovereigns, and after a time they declared that the governor had decided to let the ship proceed, and that the sailors would be released. What had led the governor to change his mind the Admiral could not tell, for he was informed by some of the men who had been ashore that the jealous King of Portugal had given orders that the adventurers should be imprisoned if they landed at any of his ports.

Soon after her crew had been restored, the *Niña* put out to sea. She was driven before the storm for several days, and then came to the coast of Portugal. Though Columbus feared the treatment he might receive from the Portuguese, he dared not proceed farther in such stormy weather, and he anchored at the mouth of the river Tagus. There the governor of a town hard by rowed out to him, and ordered him to get into the boat and give an account of himself.

But when he declared who he was, and from what great quest he had returned, he was treated more courteously, and soon King John himself sent for him and listened eagerly to his story, wondering whether the new lands could not be claimed by Portugal after all. Columbus with calm dignity assured him that the credit and glory of the expedition belonged to the Spanish sovereigns, and, though the King was greedy, he knew the adventurer was too stern a man to frighten. And so, after spending days and nights in fruitless plottings with his counsellors, in the end he was obliged to give up all that once might have been his; for he dared not risk a war with Spain.

Again Columbus set forth, and this time he steered direct for the port of Palos from which he had sailed. All the people came flocking out to meet the ship, and they were rejoiced to see their brothers and sons again. But greater still was the joy at Palos and throughout Spain when tidings came of the rich and beautiful lands that had been discovered. First Columbus' old supporters, among them the prior of the convent, came to him, and congratulated him, and made a great feast in his honour. Then he was led to the city of Seville, which he entered in triumph. Before him walked the Indians whom he had brought back, bearing baskets full of the new gold and wearing gold collars and bracelets. Other men carried specimens of strange plants and animals and brightly coloured birds; and one huge scaly lizard five feet long alarmed the crowd which thronged the streets. Nobles, priests, and merchants vied with each other in doing honour to the discoverer.

Next he went to Barcelona, where Ferdinand and Isabella were, and marched in a procession to the palace. The King and Queen rose from their thrones when they saw him, begged him to be seated, and heard his story. When they had listened to the end, all stood and sang the Te Deum. For once in his life Columbus found a reward of his labours.

No other man would have had the heroism to steer the ships across the Atlantic Ocean, the cheerfulness which kept up the hearts of his men, nor the watchful care which had brought back every member of his crew alive and well. All Europe resounded with his praises. In England,

Henry VII. and his Court declared that the discovery was not man's work: it was a miracle. A letter came from the old student Toscanelli, who was beside himself with joy at finding his belief had proved true. No one knew, however, the true greatness of the adventure. All thought, not that a vast new continent had been found, but that Columbus had reached some islands off the east coast of India. And because the islands had been found by sailing to the west, they were named the West Indies; and this name they keep to this day.

While Columbus was at the height of the royal favour, Martin Pinzon in the *Pinta* entered the port of Palos. He did not doubt that the *Niña* had perished in the storm, and that he would bring the first news of success to Spain and be the hero of the voyage. But he heard Columbus' name on every man's lips, and he was very much disappointed. Nevertheless, he sent to Ferdinand and Isabella to tell of his own adventures, and waited anxiously for a reply. When a cold letter came forbidding him to approach the Court, he was so much grieved and dismayed that he became very ill, and after a few days he died. Pinzon was a brave man and a skilful sailor, and had done much for the success of the voyage. He paid dearly enough for his disloyalty to the Admiral.

THE FATE OF THE FIRST COLONISTS

There was no difficulty in getting ships together for a second voyage. Three large vessels, attended by fourteen smaller, such as Columbus had used before, lay waiting for him in Cadiz Bay. From all sides men pressed to take part in the expedition; sailors, craftsmen, and miners, who would be useful in the new colony; monks, who were to bring the Indians to the Christian faith; and men of noble birth, who would be the companions of the Admiral, take charge of exploring parties, and, if necessary, captain the Spaniards against attacks from the natives. All were on fire with desire of glory, of riches, of adventure. As Columbus moved about the ships his appearance was hailed with joy. Everyone watched for the great leader whose courage and genius were to bring him fortune and fame. Never was there a gladder band of adventurers.

On board were stored not only provisions, but spades and ploughs, grain and vine-slips, seeds of oranges, lemons, and other fruit, and calves, goats, sheep, and fowls for the colony. There were also eight pigs, which multiplied so quickly that the islands were soon full of them, and about twenty horses for the Spanish cavalry.

Diego Columbus went with his brother, and Bartholomew wrote to say that he would follow them out. Henceforward the Admiral in all his voyages was to be surrounded by faithful kinsmen.

One thing only troubled him. Juan de Fonseca, who had been appointed by the Spanish sovereigns to find supplies and look after the welfare of the colonists, proved to be a man of irritable temper, jealous of Columbus, and disposed to do him an ill turn. He feared that, while he was in a foreign land, one powerful enemy in Spain might do much harm. So indeed it proved.

The ships touched at the Canary Islands, and then sailed steadily across the Atlantic. Columbus steered to the south of his old course, as he hoped to make new discoveries before reaching Navidad. On Sunday the 3rd of November 1493, seven weeks after they had set out, a pilot cried: "The reward! Land! I see land!" and directly afterwards six green islands were visible. These were some of the group called the Lesser Antilles, and the ships passed from one to another in search of a good harbour.

At length the Spaniards landed at the large island of Guadaloupe, and pressed inland till they came to a village. The huts were well built and airy, but they were horrified to find in all men's bones and skulls, and traces of the cooking of human flesh. The natives had fled to the woods. However, some women were found who told Columbus that they had been made prisoners and carried off from their homes by the terrible cannibal Caribs, who inhabited this and all the smaller islands. These Caribs came in canoes, and burned the villages of the gentler Indians, killed the men and took away their bodies for food, and kept the women prisoners, for women's flesh made them sick.

The Spaniards, disgusted by this story, went back to the ships. On the way they gathered pine-apples for the first time, and declared this was the best fruit men had ever eaten. That evening they missed a captain and eight sailors, and were much alarmed lest the Caribs should have seized them. The island was too large to search, but the Admiral gave orders that guns should be fired and trumpets sounded to recall the stragglers, who still did not appear. His fears were somewhat relieved by hearing from an Indian woman that most of the Carib men were away with their king in canoes, and that those who remained had only tortoiseshell arrows, and were no match for the Spaniards.

After a day or two had passed, and no news had come, Ojeda, a brave young noble, offered to lead an expedition in search of the lost party. But though he climbed up rocky hills and through almost impassable gorges, he saw no traces of them. At last, on the fourth day, after all hope had been given up, the wanderers arrived, dirty and exhausted. They said they had met no savages, but had strayed through forests where the trees were so tall and thick that they could not see the sun in the daytime nor the stars by night. They would have died if they had not by chance come to the sea and followed it round the island to the ships. Columbus punished the men severely for lingering behind, and then set sail without having seen the war-bands of Guadaloupe.

Later, however, he did fight with the Caribs. A boat's crew came upon a canoe filled with men and women of a yellowish colour, long-haired, and with their ankles and wrists so tightly bound by cotton bandages that their legs and arms were dreadfully swollen. At first they were startled by the approach of the white men, and sat still; then, as they drew nearer, they turned on them fiercely, instead of running away as the other Indians did, and shot some of the Spaniards with poisoned arrows. They were made prisoners and put in chains, but even then they glared at their captors with such threatening looks that they were terrible to approach. No gentleness and no bribes could soften either the men or the women, and Columbus, who naturally was horrified by their cannibal habits, soon gave up his attempts.

Fearing that the colonists might be getting short of provisions, he determined not to delay longer among these islands, but to sail to the north-west for Hayti. He reached the eastern point and passed slowly along the north coast, looking out for signs of his old crew. Before reaching Navidad he had to cross the mouth of the Golden River, a great stream which flowed from the very heart of the island. There some of his men who had gone ashore made a horrible discovery. Four corpses bound with grass-ropes were lying in the sun. One had a beard, and they knew him to be a Spaniard, for all the Indians had smooth chins.

A great fear fell upon the expedition, and they moved on in dread of some shameful disaster. At night they reached Navidad, and found all quiet and dark. Guns were fired, but there was no answering report from the shore. The sailors stared into the dusk, but could distinguish nothing, and Columbus would not let them leave the ships till morning. After some hours a few Indians in a canoe hailed the vessels. They brought two masks of gold as a present to Columbus from Guacanagari, who, they said, was wounded.

The Admiral asked them many questions about the welfare of the fort. Slowly and unwillingly they answered that some of the Spaniards had died of disease, and others had fought among themselves for gold, and perished. The rest were well. On being further pressed, they confessed that two Indian princes from the south had attacked the white men, and that the fort had been destroyed. Guacanagari, they declared, had received his wound fighting to defend the colonists. Much distressed, Columbus dismissed the Indians, and they left the ship.

On the next day a boat's crew was landed and found the settlement destroyed. The stockade was broken down, the fort was level with the ground, and grass grew on the roofs of the huts. Not far away was an Indian village, from which the natives fled at their approach. They searched the empty houses, and found several articles belonging to their unhappy countrymen, among them a costly cloak and some stockings. Farther away still they came upon eleven graves, not long made, but already covered with grass. Not one Spaniard could they find to tell the true tale of the disaster. All must be dead.

Filled with anger, the sailors returned and begged the Admiral to lead them against the faithless Indians at once. He refused, saying that he was not yet certain of their guilt. The men said bitterly, "What, then, has changed the nature of the Indians if not this horrible crime? Formerly they came to us with gifts. Now whole villages are deserted before us." But Columbus shook his head, not knowing what to think.

Before dinner he went on shore with all his officers to visit Guacanagari. The chief, who was lying in a hammock, complained of the pain in his leg; but, with tears in his eyes, expressed his joy at seeing his dear brother again. Columbus insisted that he should show his wound to the Spanish surgeon, and, while the native seemed unwilling, he could not refuse. To every one's astonishment, when the leg was unwrapped it looked perfectly whole and sound, though Guacanagari moaned loudly whenever it was touched. Columbus was very doubtful of the Indian's honesty, but on all sides were signs that the tribe really had been attacked and plundered by another band of Indians, and he thought it better for the present to remain on good terms with his old friend. So he bade him a kindly farewell and returned on board.

There a storm of reproach awaited him. The monks, headed by a certain Father Boil, were especially fierce in their outcry. Why did he not put to death this traitor who had killed his followers? Was it for his private ends that he passed over such a deed? How much had the Indian paid him as a bribe?

However, the Admiral went his own way without over-much explanation to the Spaniards, and during the next week, by inquiry among the Indians, he learned the true history of the fort. The colonists had become discontented for two reasons, first, because the air in the marshy district round Navidad was unhealthy, and they had suffered from fever, and then because they all wanted gold and could get none in the neighbourhood. Many of them rebelled against their leaders and marched to Cibao, the gold country of the interior, where they were murdered by the natives. The rest remained in the fort, sick, or idle, or employing their time in annoying the friendly Indians. At last, the chiefs of the Cibao, who had destroyed their comrades, marched against them also, and though Guacanagari had tried to assist them, he had been driven back, while the white men were massacred.

Saddened by this story, Columbus worked hard to regain the confidence of the Indians. He did not know that this was only the beginning of the unhappy history of the conquest of the West Indies, that before long the whole of the Indians would have died under the rods and swords of the Spaniards, and that thousands of Spaniards would fall victims to their own greed, cruelty, and pride. "To these quiet lambs," said a wise historian, writing of the natives, "to these quiet lambs, with such blessed qualities, came the Spaniards like most cruel tigers, wolves, and lions, enraged with a sharp and tedious hunger; for these forty years past minding nothing else but the slaughter of these unfortunate wretches, whom with diverse kinds of tortures, neither seen nor heard of before, they have cruelly butchered."

THE SETTLEMENT OF ISABELLA

In order to soothe Guacanagari's alarm, Columbus invited him to dinner on board. The poor chief, who had been so much afraid that he dared not meet the Spaniards without binding up a false wound, was delighted by this kindness, and went readily. As he roamed about the ship looking at different things, he met some of the Indian women who had been rescued from the Caribs. With one tall beautiful girl he talked earnestly for a long time, and she seemed unwilling to let him go. That night the women leapt overboard and swam ashore; a few were recaptured, but six escaped to Guacanagari, who retreated with his tribe into the forest, and was not seen by the Spaniards for some time. The Admiral was somewhat hurt by the chief's conduct, although he saw it was due to goodwill towards the captives, and his followers vowed vengeance if Guacanagari fell into their hands.

They now set about choosing the site for the new city. The animals could no longer be kept on board, the grain should be sown, the men were impatient at being cooped up in the ships.

Some fifty miles to the east of Navidad they found a good harbour, where two rivers ran into the sea. There was a smooth beach between the streams, behind which lay a pile of rocks which would serve as the base of a fort. The sea teemed with fish. On the banks of one river was a thick wood through which a rabbit could scarcely make its way. The ground on the other river was easily cleared, and quantities of wheat, barley, sugar-canes, and vines were planted. These grew fast. The church and the fortress must be built of stone, but ordinary dwellings were made in native fashion of timber and reeds. So well did the set-tlers work that in January 1494 they were able to sleep ashore in their new city Isabella, named after their Queen.

But alas! no sooner had they begun to settle down than fever broke out. Columbus fancied that the sick-ness was caused by the lack of fresh food; the new crops were not yet ready for harvest, the bread and wine they had brought with them were bad, and there was no meat, since they dared not kill the few animals they had. He determined to despatch some of the vessels to Spain for provisions, especially for calves and sheep, but he must send in them a cargo of gold, and hitherto he had not had time to seek for it.

However, Cibao was only four days' march from Isa-bella, and since Columbus did not wish to leave the new city himself, he allowed Ojeda to lead a party to the gold country. Ojeda and his companions, overjoyed by their good fortune, set off across a beautiful plain, through which the Golden River flowed, up to the hills of Cibao. They were amused to hear the Indians cry out in dismay at the new monsters, for they thought the riders and their horses were some horrible animals. But when the Spaniards dismounted they soon calmed the fears of these people, and they heard glowing accounts of the gold bars and nuggets, which were, as always, in some far district. Nevertheless they saw gold enough to satisfy them glittering in the sands of the streams, and Ojeda picked up one virgin nugget which weighed half a pound.

With this they returned to Columbus, who sent all the specimens he could collect, both of gold and of the fruits and spices of the island, to Spain. He wrote that this was but a promise for the future, and that he would begin immediately to mine for gold. And he asked the King and Queen whether it would not be wise to capture as many of the cruel Caribs as possible and to use them as slaves to till the land and dig for gold.

Now for this last proposal Columbus has been much blamed, because thus he brought slavery into the New World. It is true that he was the first to advise it; yet at that time white men everywhere made slaves of the darker races. Columbus, too, was always kind to the friendly Indians; it was only the cannibal Caribs that he hated and wished to keep under restraint.

Soon after the ships had sailed the Admiral was taken ill. Some of the unruly Spaniards, who disliked being governed by a foreigner from Genoa, gathered together, declared that all Columbus' words were vain, that there was no gold in Hayti, and that they would seize a ship and tell their countrymen in Spain the truth. Fortunately Columbus recovered in time to hear of the plot and to throw the plotters into chains. It seems that no one else in the colony had courage to interfere.

Then he set out on his journey to Cibao, followed by about four hundred men, mostly miners and craftsmen, and with Ojeda and his companions to guide him and clear a way through the forest. He marvelled at the lovely country as Ojeda had done; he was well received by the Indians, who brought presents of bread and fruit, and he found gold scattered in the beds of the streams.

He set some of his men to wash for gold by catching the water in shallow trays in which it dropped its dust, others to dig deeper into the earth, and still others to build a fortress to protect the miners whom he might leave in this lonely spot. When the citadel was ready, he named it Fort St. Thomas, set Ojeda in charge of it, and returned to Isabella.

There he was sorely needed. Fever had broken out again, food was running short, the Spaniards, free from his firm rule, had begun to ill-treat the natives, who ceased to bring fruit and vegetables to the settlement. All were discontented. Columbus could no longer be patient with the lazy adventurers. He made a stern decree. Every man must work with his hands, till the ground, grind corn, or do something useful to the colony. If any one refused, he should not eat. The angry Spaniards, who had been taught to think work shameful, protested in vain against these harsh orders. Father Boil cried that monks were sent to do higher and nobler things than toil in the fields; he was told that monks should then have only half rations of food. Unwillingly they all fell to work, and for the time the colony was saved, but Columbus had made many bitter enemies, who would not be long without their revenge.

Yet then all seemed to be going well, and he decided that he might leave the colony for a short time. His brain was full of the new lands waiting for him to find them, of the great cities of Asia governed by powerful kings who would hail him as a messenger from the east. He had been bound in Hayti long enough. His part in life was not to govern one peaceful island, but to discover an empire.

He left Isabella in charge of a council, at whose head sat Diego Columbus. Ojeda was to remain in command at Fort St. Thomas, and Margarit, another daring officer, was to explore the island, keeping on good terms with the friendly Indians, and if possible to frighten the great chief Caonabo, who hated the Spaniards and had caused the massacre at Navidad. Columbus feared no real danger from the natives, for just before his departure one Spanish horseman had been able to rescue five Spaniards from a mob of five hundred Indians.

He set sail to the west, and as he passed the ruins of Navidad he stopped to see if he could hear anything of Guacanagari. But the chief hid in the woods, and the ships proceeded on their course. They soon reached the eastern point of Cuba.

Columbus was very anxious to know whether this land was an island like the others he had explored, or, as he hoped, part of a great continent. He turned along the southern coast and soon saw villages with smoke coming from them, and fires blazing on the shore. When he landed the natives fled, but left behind them a banquet of fish, lizards, and vegetables, most of which the Spaniards ate eagerly, though they refused the lizards. They spoke to one Indian who lingered on a rock above the shore, and explained that they would pay for what they had taken. He assured them that his people would not take pay, that in one night they could catch as much as the white men had eaten, and bade them a friendly good-bye. Later, the natives they met were less timid, and were full of good-will. They brought many gifts, and, when asked if they had gold, smiled and pointed to the south. The Admiral determined to follow their direction, and after two days reached the island of Jamaica.

Here he was received differently. A number of war-canoes, manned by natives painted black, and shaking spears, came in pursuit of the ships, and, though he out-sailed them, when he anchored he found more opposition. The beach was covered with Indians hurling their spears into the water and uttering cries of rage. The men went ashore well armed and let fly a shower of arrows which killed many natives. They then unchained a great dog, and the Indians fled in dismay. Seeing no gold, Columbus got fresh water and left the island, though not before he had won the friendship of the savages. One young man even went with him on his voyage.

He reached Cuba again, but it became difficult to persevere on a western course. The weather was stormy and treacherous, the sea was full of islands and sunken rocks, and sailing became very dangerous. The natives all declared that the land had no end, that a man could march for many days to the west and still go on, and the sailors began to murmur that no island was ever so large as this great country. The ships' bottoms were foul and took in water, the masts creaked and groaned, the rigging was worn. It was necessary to return, and at a point where the coast bent suddenly towards the south-west the Admiral decided to do so.

He was over-tired by continual watching, and had hardly recovered from his illness at Isabella, and so for a very sensible man he did a very foolish thing. He made everybody on the ships, down to the smallest cabin-boy, sign a paper to say that Cuba was not an island but part of the mainland, and he threatened that any one who ever denied this should receive a hundred lashes and have his tongue cut out. This paper was taken from ship to ship and solemnly signed by every member of the crew. All were ignorant that a two days' sail would have brought them to the end of Cuba and showed them the sea beyond. And so they went back with their precious document.

Columbus took the same course for his return voyage. He was driven out of his way by storms and touched at Jamaica again; then the ships were separated by the winds, but joined at a point on the south of Hayti. They explored the coast here until Columbus fell suddenly into a deep swoon, and his men feared death was at hand. They carried him as quickly as might be to Isabella, which he reached unconscious.

Little had been done by this expedition; Columbus had found Jamaica and fallen into error about Cuba. But much had happened to injure the colony while he was away.

TROUBLE IN HAYTI

Margarit, who was over the army, was a brave and proud officer who would not readily obey any man. To Christopher Columbus he had been faithful, awed by his dignity and charmed by his enthusiasm, but for the quiet, patient Diego Columbus he had no respect. As the head of the armed Spaniards he began to think himself master of the island, and to take no orders from Isabella. He was encouraged by Father Boil and some nobles whom Columbus had offended, and together they would have marched against the city, if the older and more masterful brother, Bartholomew Columbus, had not arrived with a small fleet. It was too late to draw back; they dared not openly attack Diego now that he was supported by a man of proved courage and ability; so the band of discontented Spaniards seized the vessels in the harbour and sailed to Spain, resolved there to do what harm they might to Columbus' fame.

Meanwhile, the army without its leader broke up. In small bodies the men went their own way, robbing and insulting the Indians, who soon rose against them under the great chief Caonabo. He was a warrior of Carib blood, and was noted for his bravery as well as his skill in war.

His country beyond Cibao was defended by steep rocky hills and thick forests, and he was adored by his men. The Indians of his tribe rushed upon the scattered Spaniards and killed them all. Then a bolder thought entered Caonabo's mind: he resolved to attack the Spaniards in their own forts and rid the island of them.

In Fort St. Thomas Ojeda stood firm. He had his men under control, and allowed them to leave the shelter of the walls only in strong parties which easily beat off the lightly armed Indians. Caonabo besieged the fort with ten thousand men, and attempted to starve out its defenders. But every day the gates opened, and a band of Spaniards, headed by Ojeda, drove back the foremost of the natives. The two heroes seemed born to meet each other in battle. Ojeda believed that he had a charmed life, for in all the fights in which he had taken part he had not received a scratch, and the Indians learned to believe it too when they saw arrows and spears turn aside from him, and they shrank from his strong right arm. Like Caonabo, he was beloved by his followers.

Once during the siege a friendly Indian managed to get into Fort St. Thomas. He brought two wood-pigeons for Ojeda, who saw his officers look at them hungrily. "Alas," said he, "there is not enough to feed us all; they must go;" and he opened the window and let them fly.

After three months Caonabo was forced to retreat from the fort by the loss of his bravest warriors.

Thus, when Columbus returned, the island was in

a tumult, which Diego was unable to quell because he lacked decision and courage, and Bartholomew because he had no authority.

As soon as he had recovered from his swoon, Columbus was visited by Guacanagari, who told him that the chiefs of the island had banded together against the Spaniards, and that because he had refused to take part in the plot against his dear friend Columbus, his own life was in danger. The Admiral was delighted to find that his old comrade was faithful, and thanked him warmly for the news. He then gave full powers to Bartholomew to crush the revolt.

Ojeda also came to greet Columbus, and declared that with the help of ten men he would make Caonabo a prisoner. He set off on this daring adventure at once. The Indians had great reverence for the sound of a bell, and would listen for hours to the one in the church in Isabella, saying that it must have fallen from the skies. By promising this bell to Caonabo, Ojeda tempted him to leave his own country and come within its sound. He then showed the chief a set of steel fetters polished until they shone like silver, and told him that they were worn by the Spanish princes on festival days. Caonabo wished to try them on; and Ojeda proposed that he should bathe in the river, and then mount the Spaniard's horse and wear the brilliant ornaments. Caonabo, delighted by his enemy's generosity, agreed willingly, got on horseback for the first time, and put on the fetters. Immediately

Ojeda sprang up behind him and rode off with him a helpless prisoner. He was taken to Isabella and brought before Columbus, whom he treated with scorn. To Ojeda, on the other hand, he showed all possible respect, saying that he was a brave and cunning enemy, who had with his own hands captured Caonabo.

The other chiefs were easily defeated. One battle indeed was fought, but the Spanish horses broke through the lines of Indians, and in their flight they were pursued by bloodhounds. All parts of the island were now put under strict guard. Forts were built everywhere, and the Indians were forced to pay a tax of gold-dust. In some districts gold could not be found, and the unhappy people were cruelly whipped; in others the Indians were not used to work, and pined away under their new labours. Thousands of them died, the once peaceful villages fell into ruins, and yet Columbus dared not take off the harsh tax, for he knew that only by sending treasure could he satisfy Spain.

Even as it was, things were going badly with him at Court. The slanders of Margarit and Father Boil against "the upstart foreigner from Genoa" had gained some ground, and though Diego Columbus arrived at Seville with a large quantity of gold and five hundred natives to be sold as slaves, he did not win the royal favour. Isabella forbade the sale of the Indians, and ordered them to be sent back to their homes, and both monarchs agreed that it would be well to ask one of their own officers to go out and report to them on the state of the colony.

Unfortunately the man they chose was vain and obstinate, and interfered so much with Columbus that the latter decided to return home to plead his own cause. He made Bartholomew governor in his stead, ordered him to search for gold in the south of Hayti, and, if possible, to build a city there, and then set out for Spain.

This was an unfortunate and miserable voyage. Two small ships carried the sick, the discontented, and the idle of the colony. East winds delayed the passage until the provisions were almost exhausted, and daily rations of six ounces of bread and a pint of water were served out to each man. Columbus was tired and ill, and could not cheer his mournful crew; murmurs of every sort arose; the men believed the vessels had wandered from their true course; in their hunger they wished to kill and eat the Indians, who were themselves terrified and sea-sick. Caonabo, who was being brought to Spain to be shown as the captive king of the island, died on the way. At length land was sighted, and the wretched band of adventurers landed at Cadiz.

There was little enthusiasm to greet Columbus. Men's hopes of untold treasure had already been disappointed, and the stories of Margarit and his followers had spread abroad. Ferdinand and Isabella nevertheless received him kindly, and promised help in any new voyages he might make. He was entertained at many splendid banquets, of one of which the following story is told.

An envious courtier listening to Columbus' talk

observed that after all there was nothing very wonderful in what he had done. Any of those present could have sailed across the ocean in a direct course; any of them therefore could have discovered the Indies. The Admiral took an egg and asked which of them could make it stand on its end. It was passed from hand to hand round the table, while all declared that it was impossible. Columbus tapped the bottom of the egg against the table, and, crushing it slightly, balanced it. "We could have done that," said the courtiers eagerly. "So could you have discovered the Indies, when I had led the way," was the reply.

But it was not for feasts and entertainments that Columbus had come; and there was no money forthcoming for another voyage, for the Spanish sovereigns at that time needed all they had. For two years he waited, sick at heart and cursing the delay, while bad and good news in turn came from his colony. At length the King and Queen had leisure to attend to their most famous servant, and preparations were made for a third voyage, this time not to find a mere island, but to pass beyond to the great continent of America itself.

The Third Voyage

Queen Isabella had always been Columbus' staunch friend. She saw clearly that even if there were, as was now generally believed, but little gold in the islands, that the Spanish Crown, which already owed so much to Columbus, might gain more glory through new discoveries. She also hoped to do something for the Indians. Accordingly she gave orders that eight ships should be provided, furnished with all Columbus required, that five hundred of her subjects might proceed to the colony, and that Juan de Fonseca should give all possible help to the Admiral.

Nevertheless there was great difficulty in finding men willing to embark. So mournful had been the tidings brought by the adventurers who had returned, and so wretched and sallow had been their appearance, that men shrank from the enterprise. Columbus was forced to take prisoners who had served part of their sentence, and other base men. These, of course, did much harm in the colony.

Fonseca took pleasure in hindering the preparations in every possible way. He had always hated Columbus, and it was only in these petty things that he dared show his spite. One of his servants was so rude and lazy that the Admiral lost his temper and kicked the man out of the ship. The tale that Columbus had kicked and ill-treated a Spanish officer was promptly carried to Ferdinand and Isabella, and unfortunately they thus learned to think of him as a man of violent temper.

Columbus sailed on his third voyage with six ships, for two had been sent on to the colony with provisions. He soon gave orders to three more to steer directly to Hayti, while with the other three he turned to the south. He had come to believe that he would find the mainland more easily, and escape the host of islands, if he kept nearer to the Equator. Moreover, he had been told that gold and precious stones would be found plentifully only where the sun's rays were hottest, and that the people of those favoured lands would be black with woolly hair as they were in Africa, instead of being brown and straight-haired like his Indians.

He touched at the Canary Islands and the Cape Verde Islands, and soon found himself in the region of the Equator. It was stiflingly hot; the sun glared all day upon the decks, making the tar bubble in the seams of the planks, and spoiling the food. Columbus wrote in a letter to Spain: "I entered a climate where the intensity of the heat was such that I thought both ships and men would have been burnt up, and everything suddenly got into such a state of confusion that no man dared go below deck to attend to the securing of the water-cask and the provisions. This heat lasted eight days." As they advanced westward, however, the weather grew milder, and refreshing breezes blew, and at last three mountains were seen rising in the centre of an island. The Admiral was surprised to find this a green, well-watered land, for he had expected all countries so far south to be dry and parched. He gave it the name of Trinidad (Trinity) on account of its three hills.

As he passed along the south coast of Trinidad on the 1st of August 1498, he saw land in the distance which he took for another island. But really this was his first glimpse of the mainland of America, and the land he saw was the part of South America at the mouth of the river Orinoco. So that here truly for the first time Columbus discovered America, though he did not know it. He sailed up the channel between Trinidad and the continent for a good many days. At both ends of the channel he was nearly shipwrecked, for the water seethed and tossed in its haste to pass the capes. Because these passages were so dangerous he called them the Serpent's Mouth and the Dragon's Mouth, and he resolved not to venture there again.

The Indians of this district were fairer, and wore more clothing than those he had met before. Columbus was surprised, for he had expected them to be negroes; and he could only suppose that there was some change in the shape of the earth which made that region cooler than it otherwise would have been. He thought about the matter for a long time, and came to the clever but mistaken conclusion that, instead of being round, the world was pear-shaped, and that he had come to the place where the stalk of the pear should be. So even though the place lay on the Equator, it was on a mountain, and for that reason cool.

The Admiral tried to find a way into the sea among the islands in order not to pass through the Dragon's Mouth, but the land hindered him in every direction, and the Indians told him it was impossible. He noticed that many of their women wore necklaces of pearls, as well as gold ornaments. These pearls they obtained from the oysters in that gulf, which they called Paria. As the shores appeared to be covered with oysters, he was delighted with thoughts of the new treasures that would swell the King of Spain's hoards.

He left Trinidad by the Dragon's Mouth, and came to an island where he saw Indians diving for pearls. He bought a great many in exchange for gay china and bells, and would have stopped longer had he not suddenly fallen ill and become completely blind for a time. There was nothing for it but to sail to Hayti in hope of finding rest for his body and mind.

But trouble had again broken out in the island. For a time Bartholomew Columbus had kept order with a firm hand; but while he was building San Domingo, the new city, a plot was made in Isabella against him. Roldan, a proud, daring, and unscrupulous Spaniard, gathered round him discontented men of all ranks; they broke into the storehouses for weapons and provisions, and marched into the unexplored part of Hayti, where they spent their time in various pleasures. Not only did Roldan defy the Government: he began to stir up a revolt among the Indian chiefs. Bartholomew Columbus was not sure of the loyalty of his followers; he dared not lead them against their countrymen; but he did put down the Indian rebellion.

When the Admiral arrived he heard tidings of disaster on every side—of lands untilled, crops ungathered, mines unworked; of the country plundered by bands of white men and natives in turn. He had not enough soldiers to attack Roldan, so he wrote to him promising that, if he came quietly to Isabella, he and his men should receive either a free pardon in the colony or a passage home. But the rebel wanted more than this; he demanded lands for his followers, and a high post for himself. These too had to be granted. Roldan then returned to the city, where he bore himself as the Admiral's equal, and even insulted him in public. Most of his men sailed for Spain.

There they swelled the outcry against Columbus. King Ferdinand had already heard accounts of the disturbances in Hayti, and had begun to doubt the Admiral's prudence. For some years he had received none of the promised gold, but only requests for more provisions, tools, and ships. Queen Isabella had been angry at the enslavement of the natives against her wishes. "By what authority does Columbus venture thus to dispose of my subjects?" she asked. Fonseca too had always repeated every ill-natured tale he could hear.

Now there arrived two ships filled with angry Spaniards, who complained of enforced work, of lack of food, of the wretched state of the country, and declared that Columbus wished to make himself King of Hayti, instead of sending its wealth to Spain. The very mob of the Spanish cities spat at the Admiral's name. Young men gathered round Diego and Fernando Columbus, and insulted those "whose father had led so many brave nobles to seek graves in the land of vanity and delusion." Ferdinand and Isabella determined to send out an officer of high rank, with full powers to do anything he thought necessary for the good of the island—power even over Columbus.

But again they made an unfortunate choice in Francis Bobadilla, who was weak and pompous, and already considered the Admiral guilty of everything that had been laid to his charge.

On arriving at Isabella Bobadilla's eyes fell on the bodies of some Spanish rebels hanging on a gibbet. Horrified at this sight, he called for an explanation, and listened eagerly to every complaint brought against the Admiral. He ordered that Diego Columbus, who was then in the city, should be bound and imprisoned, he took possession of the Admiral's house and all his goods and papers, and he sent to bid him at once come to the town.

Columbus at first refused, not believing in Bobadilla's authority, but obeyed when he was shown the royal letters.

He went unarmed before the new governor, who, without respect either for his rank or for the services he had rendered to the Spanish Court, ordered him to be put into chains. Silence fell upon the attendants, all gazed upon the stern and majestic figure of the fallen governor, and no one moved to obey. Bobadilla repeated his order, but his men were unwilling to have part in such a shameful deed. He offered a reward, and after some minutes a low cook stepped forward, who was ready to do anything for money. Then in the midst of the hushed gathering this fellow fastened on the fetters, and the prisoner was removed, calm and dignified, though ignorant what his fate would be.

Bobadilla was afraid that Bartholomew Columbus would take up arms; he ordered his prisoner to request his brother to give himself up. Columbus said he would obey the royal command in this also, and Bartholomew was put in irons.

The Admiral and his brothers were then confined on one of the ships in the harbour. They were not allowed to see each other, but were left to expect death. Meanwhile Bobadilla set to work to collect every sort of charge against them from the vilest Spaniards in the place. One man was found to declare that Columbus had kept for himself a sack of pearls which he should have sent to Spain; another that he had hidden a treasure of gold; others that he had starved and ill-treated his Spanish followers; and still others that he had tortured Indians to death. Bobadilla in great delight wrote down all these reports, and then, because he dared not execute the Admiral himself, resolved to send him and his brothers home for punishment.

Vallejo, captain of one of the vessels at Isabella, was ordered to take them on board. He went to the Admiral, saluted him, and begged him to accompany him.

"Vallejo, where are you leading me?" said the prisoner gravely, thinking the orders for his murder had come.

"On board, sir."

"Is this true, Vallejo?"

"On my honour, sir," said the captain, "you are to come on board my ship."

And Columbus followed, believing that when he came to Spain his cause would be safe in the hands of the King and Queen.

When he had been at sea a few hours Vallejo begged him to let him remove the chains, for there was now nothing to fear from Bobadilla. But the proud adventurer would not allow this. "No," he said, "I wear them by the King of Spain's orders; I shall wear them until he has me released." And all through the voyage, in spite of his own health and Vallejo's pleadings, he continued to wear them.

He felt his disgrace bitterly, and in a letter which he wrote to a friend at Court he said, "I have now reached that point that there is no man so vile but thinks it his right to insult me. The governor on his arrival at Hayti took up his abode in my house and made use of all that was there. Well and good; perhaps he was in want of it, but even a pirate does not behave in this way to the merchant whom he plunders." And he declared indignantly, "I am judged in Spain as a governor who had been sent to a city under regular government, and in this I receive enormous wrong. I ought to be judged as a captain sent from Spain to the Indies to conquer a nation numerous and warlike, a captain who for so many years has borne arms, never quitting them for a moment. If twelve years' hardships and fatigues, if continual dangers and frequent famines, if the ocean first opened and five times passed and repassed to add a new world abounding with wealth to the Spanish monarchy, if an infirm old age brought on by these services deserve these chains as a reward, it is very fit I should wear them to Spain and keep them by me as memorials to the end of my life."

As soon as the ships reached Spain, this letter was sent to the sovereigns, and both were moved with indignation when they heard of the treatment their great servant had received. They ordered that the brothers should be set free at once, that all honour should be shown to them, and that they should come to Court as soon as possible. But, when the fetters were removed, Columbus had them nailed on to his cabin wall, where he might always see them; and he made his friends promise that, when he died, they should be buried with him.

Then he went before the King and Queen, a grey-haired, bent old man, with the story of his misfortunes and sufferings written on his wrinkled face. When Isabella saw him tears came into her eyes, and she bade him rise from his knees, but he broke down and wept. She and Ferdinand talked with him, and heard of his wonderful discovery of gold and pearls in the Gulf of Paria, and of all his labours. And they told him how angry they were that Bobadilla should have used his power so ill, and promised that he should be recalled at once. And Columbus, who could never be idle, began to dream of a new voyage, which would bring still more glory to Spain.

The Fourth Voyage

A Spanish noble, Ovando, was sent out to Hayti as Governor, with orders to dismiss Bobadilla, and to claim from him all the property stolen from Columbus. He was commanded to make as much haste as possible, because it was certain that Bobadilla was ruling the island very badly, and that the Indians were suffering ill-treatment from the colonists, who used them as if they were cattle. Columbus asked to be sent out himself, but he was told that Ovando must first have time to get the island under control, and that then he would again be made Governor.

Therefore he gave his mind to the new adventure. He had noticed, while he was out in Paria, that a great current of water passed along to the west. Now he knew that this current must find some outlet for itself, and there was no such passage among the West Indian Islands which he had explored; so he fancied there must be some strait north of Paria through which the water escaped. For, because he thought Cuba was part of the mainland, he did not imagine that the water might find its way to the west of that island, as it does in the mighty Gulf Stream. And Columbus believed that, if there were such a strait, he might surely bring a ship through it, and, sailing on, come perhaps to new countries, perhaps to India, perhaps right round the world to Spain.

Queen Isabella listened to him favourably, for she always trusted in the justness of his reasoning; and four small ships were given to him. Bartholomew Columbus tried to persuade his brother that he was not young and strong enough to go on another dangerous voyage, but insisted on going with him when his words proved useless. Fernando, Columbus' second son, now a boy of thirteen, also accompanied his father.

This expedition sailed on the 9th of May 1502, and was unfortunate from the first. One of the ships sailed so badly that the others had continually to stop and wait for it, and the Admiral determined to call at San Domingo, and try to obtain a better vessel. But Ovando sent a boat out to say that he, as Governor of Hayti, commanded the fleet to leave at once. Columbus dispatched a messenger to warn him that a storm was approaching, and to ask if he might take shelter in the harbour. This request was refused.

He then got his ships under the lee of an island, where, with bare poles, they bore the force of the winds bravely. A terrible hurricane came up, and lasted for several days, but, though injured, the little fleet was not destroyed. On the other hand, the vessels in which Bobadilla and Roldan were returning to Spain put boldly out to sea, and in a day or two all went to the bottom but one small ship, which was carrying some treasure belonging to

Columbus. Thus the Admiral's enemies perished; and people were not slow to say that God had shown His care for His true servant, while He allowed his wicked foes to drown. Columbus himself declared: "I am satisfied it was the hand of God, for had they arrived in Spain, they would never have been punished as their crimes deserved, but favoured and rewarded."

He waited a few days in a desert part of Hayti while his ships were thoroughly repaired after the storm, and then he steered for Cuba, and thence to the south-west. He soon came in sight of a pleasant island covered with pines, behind which lay the main coast. On the way he met a great canoe filled with Indians, who told him they had come from the north, from a country rich in gold, and inhabited by many thousands of people. This was the kingdom of Mexico, and if he had sailed there he would have come to a land richer than any he had imagined—the land of gold itself. But, unfortunately, he thought only of the strait he was seeking, and was resolved to turn southwards to find it.

Now South America was not at this time quite an unknown land. Not only had Columbus visited Paria, but many other men had obtained copies of his maps, or employed his seamen to guide them, and had sailed up the coast from Brazil as far as the Isthmus of Darien collecting treasure. However, none of them had come farther north, and that part of Central America which Columbus had reached was still unexplored.

As the ships sailed towards the south another terrible storm arose which lasted for six weeks. "My ships lay exposed, with sails torn, and anchors, rigging, cables, boats, and a great quantity of provisions lost," Columbus said in a letter. "My people were very weak and humbled in spirit, many of them promising to lead a religious life, and all making vows and promising to perform pilgrimages. The distress of my son who was with me grieved me to the soul, and the more when I considered his tender age, for he was but thirteen years old, and he enduring so much toil for so long a time. Our Lord, however, gave him strength even to enable him to encourage the rest, and he worked as if he had been eighty years at sea. I myself had fallen sick, and was many times at the point of death, but from a little cabin that I had caused to be constructed on the deck I directed our course. My brother was in the ship that was in the worst condition and the most exposed to danger; and my grief on this account was the greater that I brought him with me against his will."

At last the little squadron was able to reach a harbour where fresh water and provisions were obtained, and the ships overhauled. Friendly Indians spoke to Columbus of the gold of Veragua, a country not far away, but he went on in search of the western passage till he came to the Isthmus of Darien. The coast from this point to Paria had been explored by other adventurers; there was no use therefore in sailing farther. The strait did not exist; and another of his hopes had failed him.

He decided to return to Veragua to collect what gold he might, before sailing for Spain. The winds continued to rage, the ships' bottoms were bored through and through by the sea-worm, the sailors were out of health, the biscuit was bad.

However, the ships reached Veragua and anchored at the mouth of a river; the Indians were approached and presents sent to the chief Quibian. Two expeditions led inland reported that there was abundance of gold. Columbus' brain was on fire with new plans: here he would build a fort and make a settlement; here should a new colony arise which would restore the glory he had lost in Hayti. Preparations were made apace, and the Admiral decided to return to Spain for provisions and colonists, while his brother remained in charge at Veragua.

But the Indians, who were a bold and hardy race, and had from the first disliked the presence of the white strangers, resolved to make a quick end of the settlement. They gathered round Quibian in hundreds, and proposed to take the Spaniards by surprise in a night attack.

Their sullen manners were noticed by Diego Mendez, a valiant Spaniard, who resolved to ascertain the reason of their behaviour. With one companion he went in search of Quibian's village, and though he met many bands of armed Indians he was allowed to pass when he said that he was a surgeon who had come to cure a wound in Quibian's foot. He came to the royal hut, where he was less civilly treated; one of Quibian's sons rushed out angrily and threatened him with death.

Diego contrived to soothe him by showing him a looking-glass, and asking if he would not like his hair cut and arranged in the Spanish fashion. This was then done by the other Spaniard, who had some skill in the barber's art, and the vain savage allowed his enemies to depart. They reported all they had seen to the Admiral, who immediately sent seventy men to seize Quibian. The chief and his family were overpowered without the knowledge of their army, and they were led to the shore and put into a boat. As they were being rowed out, Quibian with a desperate effort freed himself from his cords, pushed into the bottom of the boat the Spaniard who was acting as his guard, and swam to the shore. There he gathered his tribesmen together and attacked the settlement fiercely.

Although Columbus was ready to sail, he had been delayed by the tides, and the savages were able to surprise a boat which he was sending to the settlement, and to kill all the crew but one man who escaped to tell the tale to Bartholomew. They then drove the defenders of the fort from its unfinished walls, and forced them to take refuge on the beach, where they made a rampart of casks and planks. Meanwhile the Admiral expected the return of the boat. He had only one other, and he dared not risk losing it, but as he became more and more anxious, a bold Spaniard volunteered to swim to land and find out what was happening.

He succeeded in doing this, and in bringing back news of the grave plight of the settlers. There was nothing for it but to take them on board, and so they were carried across, a few at a time, in the boat and in two native canoes.

All chance of establishing a colony at Veragua was at an end; the men were crowded into the two ships that remained seaworthy, and Columbus attempted to return from the most disappointing of his voyages. How exhausted he was in mind and body can be seen from his own account. "I toiled up to the highest part of the ship and with a quivering voice and fast falling tears I called upon your Highnesses' war-captains, from each point of the compass, to come to my succour; but there was no reply."

The ships reached Cuba, but were too much battered to beat up against the east wind, and Columbus headed for Jamaica. By constant use of the pumps, and even of pots and kettles, he managed to keep them above the water till they came to a sandy shore, where he ran them aground side by side, lashed them firmly together, and built huts on the decks for his men. Diego Mendez induced the natives to bring a daily supply of fresh provisions, and the sailors were fairly comfortable for the time, though they had no means of escape from the island.

After all had rested and recovered from their hardships, the Admiral sent for Diego Mendez and spoke to him as follows: "My son, not one of those whom I have here with me has any idea of the great danger in which we stand, except myself and you; for we are but few in number and these wild Indians are numerous and very fickle; and whenever they take it into their heads to come and burn us in our two ships, which we have made into straw-thatched cabins, they may easily do so by setting fire to them on the land side, and so destroy us all. The arrangement which you have made with them for the supply of food, to which they agreed with such goodwill, may soon prove disagreeable to them, and it would not be surprising if on the morrow they were not to bring us anything at all."

He then asked Diego whether he would be willing to attempt the voyage to Hayti in one of the small open canoes they could obtain from the Indians. The Spaniard hesitated. He said that he would willingly enough risk his life to bring help, but that his companions already were grumbling that the Admiral trusted him too much, and he did not wish to provoke their jealousy further. So Columbus called the men together, warned them of their danger, showed them that a message must be sent to Hayti before help could come, and asked for volunteers to undertake the enterprise. All hung back; no one would meet almost certain death. Then Diego Mendez stepped forward. "My lord," he said, "I have but one life, and I am willing to hazard it in your service and for the welfare of all those who are here with us." The Admiral arose and embraced him, kissing his cheek, and the sailors, astonished at his bravery, could only murmur words of encouragement. One of them even agreed to accompany him.

They set out bravely in two small canoes with some Indian rowers. If they gained any port in Hayti it was agreed that Diego Mendez should proceed with Columbus' letters to Spain, while his companion should return to Jamaica with provisions. Before they had gone far along the coast of that island they were stopped by some natives, but they escaped from their captors and paddled on their way undiscouraged. The weather was very hot, and on the second day the Indians became exhausted by fatigue and thirst, for their water jars were soon emptied. They lay groaning at the bottom of the boat, while the white men put up a small sail and made a little progress. One of the natives had died, and others seemed near death, when they perceived a tiny rocky island. Here they found some rain-water and a few shellfish, and thus refreshed, reached Hayti.

As soon as Diego Mendez had landed, his companion should have returned to Columbus with news of the safe arrival, but the Indians refused to tempt the seas again, and he must needs wait until some larger vessel could be procured. Diego hastened to seek Ovando, not doubting that such a ship would be immediately forthcoming. He found the governor in one of the more remote districts of the island, where he was engaged in a cruel attack on the natives. Ovando received the messenger coldly, and hardly concealed his pleasure at hearing of Columbus' misfortunes. He secretly hoped that the great founder of the colony would soon perish if he were left without ships and provisions in a distant island, and that thus he would retain the government in his own hands. Accordingly he made no attempt to help Diego, whom he put off with a few cold promises.

Therefore Columbus was left in doubt as to the fate of the canoes. The sailors became discontented, declaring that Diego Mendez was certainly drowned, and that there was no chance of rescue. They refused to obey Columbus' wise orders for exercise and care of their health. He was too infirm and miserable to control them. Finally they mutinied, and marched to another part of Jamaica, leaving only the invalids and a few faithful friends with their leader. New disasters followed. The mutineers plundered the Indians, who learned to hate all the white men, and no longer brought them food. The Spaniards on the ships were almost starving when Columbus thought of a daring and brilliant plan of bringing the savages to his feet.

He had ascertained from the calendar that there would be an eclipse of the moon one night during the next month. He therefore told the Indians that they had offended the white men's god by refusing to bring supplies, and as a punishment first the moon and then the sun would be taken from heaven, so that there would be no light left on earth. The chiefs refused to believe his words, but, when the night of the eclipse came, and a shadow appeared on the edge of the moon, they were terribly frightened, and begged him to entreat his god to pardon them. He would not consent at first, but waited until the point of total eclipse was reached and the moon was utterly darkened. Then he agreed to do his best, and they saw the shadow move slowly away, and the moon shine out once more. Such an awful threat was not to be disregarded, and henceforward the Indians were his willing servants.

When eight months had gone, a sail was seen in the distance. Ovando had sent a small ship, hoping to learn that all were dead, and to be able to report their sad end to Spain. As it was evident that the Spaniards were still alive, a boat was lowered, a man proceeded to the Admiral's ship with a piece of bacon, a cask of wine, and a letter, and without a word returned to the strange vessel, which immediately set sail. Columbus took the letter in trembling hands, and read that Ovando was sorry for his misfortunes, but was unable to offer him any help. Distressed as he was by this cruel note, Columbus at least was now aware that his followers had reached Hayti, and he was confident that Diego Mendez would not desert him. In this hope he met new attacks from the hungry mutineers. In this hope he bore up against the reproachful looks of the loyal Spaniards on the ships. And at last the expected help came.

In June 1504, a whole year after they had been wrecked on the shores of Jamaica, two ships arrived to carry away the survivors of the expedition. Henceforward their course was easy. Even Ovando could not refuse to receive the Admiral at San Domingo and to aid his passage to Spain.

And so it happened that in November 1504 Christopher Columbus returned to his adopted country for the last time.

THE DEATH OF COLUMBUS

Columbus was too ill to proceed farther than the city of Seville. There he remained while his brother, Bartholomew, and his son went on with his letters to the Court.

In these letters he spoke of Ovando's barbarity both to himself and to the natives of Hayti, and begged that he might be recalled. He asked, too, that his own claims to the government of the New World should be admitted, and that the crew which had served him for more than two years might receive their pay.

Queen Isabella had been much displeased by the story of Ovando's cruelty; she entreated the King to summon him to Spain at once. But unfortunately she died almost immediately after the Admiral's return, and thus his only powerful friend was lost to him. Ferdinand did nothing for his old servant, sick, aged, and poor as he was.

Columbus said in one letter: "I receive nothing of the revenue due to me; I live by borrowing. Little have I profited by twenty years of service with such toils and perils, since at present I do not own a roof in Spain. If I desire to eat or sleep, I have no resort but an inn, and for the most times I have not wherewithal to pay my bill."

In December he attempted the journey to Court. Ferdinand did not refuse to see him, but he grudged Columbus his offices of Viceroy and Admiral, for he was furious that so much power should have passed from the King's into the servant's hands, and he basely tried to bribe him into giving up his dignities. When the old man shook his head, and declared that the King should keep his promises and grant him what was due to him, Ferdinand made many fair speeches, promising that his demands should be looked into. He had, however, made up his mind to retain Ovando as governor, for large supplies of gold were now coming in from Hayti, and he needed wealth.

Time passed by, and Columbus began to see that he could expect nothing from the King. "It appears," he said, "that His Majesty does not think fit to fulfil that which he, with the Queen, who is now in glory, promised me by word and seal. For me to contend to the contrary would be to fight with the wind." He had won more glory for Spain than any of her own sons. He had crossed the wide Atlantic Ocean without a guide or chart. He had discovered the West Indies, the coast of South America at Paria, and nearly the whole eastern coast of Central America, and he had opened up the whole continent for other adventurers. He had ruled Hayti wisely and well, caring for the well-being of the natives and making the Spanish name honoured among them. Even in old age he had not rested, but had set out to discover new paths and lands. And in return for all this he was to die in poverty, deserted by all but a few faithful friends, not sure that any of his honours and lands would pass to his sons. For this he did what he could. In his will he declared that Diego Columbus should succeed him as Admiral of the seas and Viceroy of the Indies, and he made his friends promise to support his son's claim.

Shortly before his death he heard that the Spanish princess was returning from abroad with her husband. He was delighted by this news, believing that the daughter of Queen Isabella would be gracious to him. But he grew weaker, until he could not travel from his lodging at Valladolid to meet her, and on the 10th of May 1506 Christopher Columbus died.

His sons buried him at Seville. Diego inherited his father's title of Viceroy, and governed Hayti for eighteen years, but his children were forced to give up most of their rights. Fernando became a learned historian and wrote the life of his father.

Both sons bore on their arms the proud motto—

> "A Castilla y a Leon
> Nuevo Mundo dio Colon."

Columbus gave to Spain a New World.